L

MW00747842

Maddie in Trouble

Illustrations by Marie-Louise Gay

Translation by Sarah Cummins

First Novels

Formac Publishing Company Limited
Halifax, Nova Scotia

Formac Publishing Company Limited acknowledges the support
of the Department of Canadian Heritage and the Nova Scotia
Department of Education and Culture in the development of
writing and publishing in Canada. We acknowledge the support
of the Canada Council for the Arts for our publishing program.

Canadian Cataloguing in Publication Data

Leblanc, Louise, 1942–
    [Sophie vit un cauchemar. English]
    Maddie in trouble

    (First novel series)
    Translation of: Sophie vit un cauchemar.
    ISBN 0-88780-428-4 (pbk.)
    ISBN 0-88780-429-2 (bound)

I. Gay, Marie-Louise. II. Title. III. Series.

PS8573.E25S66613   1998   jC843'.54   C98-950055-1
PZ23.L393Ma 1998

Formac Publishing Company
Limited
5502 Atlantic Street
Halifax, NS B3H 1G4

Distributed in the U.S. by
Orca Book Publishers
P.O. Box 468 Custer, WA
U.S.A. 98240-0468

Printed and bound in Canada

Table of Contents

1
The worst day of school

Seven o'clock in the morning. Two sparrows were chirping at my bedroom window. I stretched luxuriantly. Another wonderful day of summer vacation.

Beep-beep! Beep-beep!

Was that my alarm clock? Grrr! I had forgotten that today was the first day of school.

I went downstairs a few minutes later. The kitchen was in an uproar.

Angelbaby was screaming for food. My brother Alexander was as jumpy as a nervous grasshopper. His teacher this year is

Mrs. Spiegel. She's awful! We call her Spiegel the Eagle, because she sees everything.

Alexander was checking that he had all his supplies — books, scribblers, and pencils were scattered all over the table.

"We checked it all last night!" my mother reminded him. But I understood how Alexander felt.

"With the Eagle, you can never be too careful," I said.

She turned to me, looking daggers. "Your comments were not requested, Maddie!"

"In any case," my dad laughed, "he'll lose it all as soon as he steps outside."

He didn't laugh for long. My mother gave him a withering look too. Then Angelbaby started choking. She finally spat something up. A piece of banana? Nope! Alexander's eraser!

Then my brother Julian came down, dressed in his best clothes.

"I'm ready for school," he announced, pushing his glasses up on his nose.

He was hoping to convince my parents to send him to school.

"You're too young," said my father, for the umpteenth time.

"But soon I'll be too old!" cried Julian. "Billions of blistering —"

"Let him go instead of me!" suggested Alexander. "The Eagle will make him glad he's not in school yet."

"No, it won't," said Julian. "I like eagles."

As usual, Julian was totally out of it.

My father explained the difference between eagles and the Eagle.

"There's the bus!" my mother cried. "Off you go!" Heartlessly, she pushed us out the door.

"Be good! Try to start the year out on the right foot."

As I climbed onto the bus, I tripped and banged my nose on the step.

* * *

Four o'clock in the afternoon. I felt like I was riding in an electric frying-pan. The schoolbus sizzled with laughing and shouting.

I couldn't hear myself think in all that racket. And I needed to think! Whew! The whole day had been a disaster, from start to finish.

First I found out that the Eagle was going to be *my* teacher. She moved up a grade and she didn't even have to pass the tests, like we did. That's outrageous!

So at recess I got everyone in my gang together to make a plan.

Clementine, who's the smartest kid in the class, didn't see why we needed a plan. It makes no difference to her whether she has the Eagle or some other teacher.

Nicholas was chomping down chips. He didn't have any ideas. He never does. You can't think when you're stuffing your face. And Nicholas always has a pile of snacks because his dad runs a corner store.

My brother Alexander hopped by like a grasshopper on holiday.

"Watch out! The Eagle has her eagle eye on you!" he laughed at us.

That made Patrick mad. He's the tough guy in our gang.

"Hey, pinhead!" he yelled at me. "Tell your brother to can it! Unless he wants to trade an eagle eye for a black eye!"

I didn't like being called "pinhead." Last year he called me "swell head" because I was leader of the gang.

Did he think I wasn't the leader anymore? I had to clear

this up. And I had to defend my brother too, you know!

"Don't you touch him."

"Ooooh, scary. I'm afraid," sneered Patrick.

BANG!

Nicholas had finished his chips and burst the bag.

"I fought we were talking about Misshesh Shiegal," he said with his mouth full.

"Before we do, we have to know who the leader of the gang is," said Patrick.

"My sister is!" declared Alexander.

"The strongest one should be the leader!" Patrick turned on him.

"Brute force isn't the only thing to consider," said Clementine in her little mouse voice.

I agreed with that, but not Patrick.

"Oh yeah? How are you going to defend your brother then?" he asked, giving her a shove.

Alexander was saved by the bell. I don't know how I would have answered Patrick.

"Maddie! MADDIE! We're home!"

Poor Alexander! He's going to be in serious danger if I don't come up with an answer by tomorrow morning.

I thought of Clementine. Maybe I should give her a call. She said that brute force wasn't the only thing.

But what else could there be?

2
Worries about war

At home, chaos reigned again. Angelbaby was screaming with teething pains. Julian was still living on another planet.

"I'm going to school with you! Hooray!"

"We have to wait and see what the principal says," my father cautioned.

Now I was the one who didn't get it.

"We discovered that Julian already knows how to read," explained my mother.

"And," she added proudly, "he taught himself. He's wasting his time at daycare."

"I'm not too young to go to school," declared Julian, "because I am a little genius."

My parents thought this was amusing. They have no idea. They don't know Patrick Walsh.

"You need more than genius if you're going to go to school," I told Julian. "Isn't that right, Alexander?"

"Yeah! Julian might not be too young, but he's too little."

My parents did not take these warnings to heart.

"Well, you'll be there to protect him, Maddie!"

Great! Now I had to protect both Alexander and Julian. I

figured I'd better phone Clementine right away.

"Hello, everyone!"

Gran! What was she doing
there? She was dressed in her
bicycling outfit and helmet.

"You're not ready!" she said to me.

"Ready for what?"

"We have to train for Saturday! The anti-war bike protest! Didn't we agree?"

"No!" Alexander protested. "On Saturday, I get Maddie's bike. This has been arranged for ages. And anyway, Maddie can't ride a bike worth beans."

"If she practises, she'll manage."

"It's too complicated, Gran. And anyway, before I can stop other people's war, I have to stop my own."

I hoped my parents would get the hint. I hoped they would be worried and ask me questions! But no. The only reaction I got was from Gran. She was disappointed in me. She thought I had a selfish attitude.

"You have no idea what real war is like, Maddie."

"Yes, I do! I've seen pictures on TV. There's airplanes dropping bombs."

"Have you thought about the people who are down below? About how they must feel? Their terror and suffering, after the bombs have destroyed everything?"

No, I hadn't thought about that. Gran is right. I am selfish. I'm only interested in my own petty little problems. I was ashamed of myself.

But I didn't say so. I just said, "I'll go get my bike helmet."

* * *

Gran and I rode our bikes for a long time without talking. I was thinking about what she had said.

My legs hurt. And then I fell off my bike. But I got up without complaining.

"You're doing great, honey," whispered Gran.

I felt brave. I felt as if I was accomplishing something important.

Before we went in Gran said, "So what's this about your war, Maddie?"

"Oh, it's so...insignificant compared to..."

"No war is insignificant, Maddie."

So I told her. And then the two of us concocted a plan to

make peace with Patrick. It was
a good plan. Because I was sure
I would win...

3
Peace plan abandoned

"I'm ready to fight," I announced.

Patrick burst out laughing. "Ha! Ha! You haven't got a chance."

I repeated the words Gran had used.

"We'll have a democratic battle."

"Demo-what?" said Patrick warily.

"An election," explained Clementine. "The winner is the one who gets the most votes."

"Who gets to vote?" asked Patrick, still suspicious.

"Everyone in the gang. That's what democratic means."

"Even Alexander? That's not fair! He'll just vote for his sister!"

"Not necessarily," put in Alexander.

Hmm...Alexander is sneakier than I thought. I know he'll vote for me!

Blowing and bursting bubblegum, Nicholas piped up, "POP! I don't know who to vote for either. POP!"

I couldn't believe it! Now Nicholas couldn't decide between Patrick and me. It looked like I wasn't going to win as easily as I thought,

"The candidates have to persuade us to vote for them," Clementine explained. "For example, they can make promises."

"No problem," said Patrick. "I promise to protect everyone. If you don't vote for me, you're toast. I'm stronger than everyone else."

How depressing! I felt as if I was right back where I was

yesterday. What could I promise that would beat that?

I was beginning to panic, when Clementine spoke up again.

"You'll have to come up with a better promise than that, Patrick. You're not the strongest. I am!" she announced, in all seriousness.

Patrick shrieked with laughter.

"You? A girl? Stronger than me!? You're nothing but a little mouse!"

Then Clementine went wild.

She gave out a bloodcurdling yell and pirouetted twice. Her foot slashed the air. And then she kicked Patrick on the leg and he went down like a ton of bricks.

"Karate. Yellow belt," Clementine panted. "I took lessons this summer."

Everyone was dumbfounded. I was so relieved I couldn't speak either.

"Okay," said Clementine. "Back to the elections."

"But now I really don't know who to vote for. POP! If we

don't vote for the strongest one, then how do we decide? POP!"

I thought that maybe the chief should be the smartest person in the class, but I kept my mouth shut. Except for art, I'm not much better than Patrick.

He finally got to his feet, rubbing his back. There was a weird smile on his face. I didn't like it.

"Maddie," he said, "I propose we have a contest."

"A bicycle race," suggested Alexander.

Honestly! He knows I'm hopeless on a bike. I'd lose for sure! The traitor! So he wasn't being sneaky before. Even my own brother wasn't on my side. What was going on?

Oh...he was mad because I wouldn't lend him my bike for Saturday. How selfish can you get! He should have tried to understand what I'm doing and support my anti-war protest!

He had no idea what war is like. Well, he'd soon find out!

I thought that Alexander should not be entitled to vote. First of all, he's too young. And second, it's unfair to Patrick. It is! The others would see that I wanted to win in a fair fight!

"I would like to —"

Patrick interrupted me, because he thought I was going to side with Alexander.

"A bike race is a stupid idea. We need a more challenging test. A true leader is afraid of nothing."

"Whoa, Patrick! POP! So what test do you propose?"

"A test of courage: we have to steal something from a store."

This got a reaction out of everyone. They were all either totally for or totally against the idea.

If we had to vote on this, we'd never get anywhere. Anyway, it was war, right?

"I accept."

Silence fell. Then I began to think about it. Uh-oh.

4
Any colour will do!

Lunchtime. The whole gang is at the mall. Patrick has just gone into All for You, a huge department store. He stops at a counter here and there, turns down an aisle, then disappears from view.

POP! Scrootch scrootch...

GRRR! Nicholas is driving me crazy with his chewing gum!

"Do you think you could stop chewing your cud like a cow?"

"No way! I'm a nervous wreck."

"Oh, put a sock in it! YOU have nothing to be nervous about anyway."

"That's right," said Alexander. "SHE's the one who should be nervous."

"You, Two-Face," I say, "spare me your two cents' worth."

Alexander looks downcast. Ever since we got to the mall, I've been rude to everyone. I've been talking and acting just like Patrick. It's as if I'm turning into Patrick.

My nerves are shot. My stomach is in a knot. It feels as if I just swallowed a whole bowl of congealed cold spaghetti in one go.

"What's he doing in there?" Clementine asks anxiously.

"Here he comes!" cries Nicholas. "I knew he'd do it."

"He just has to get through the door!"

We all step back, ready to take off at the slightest sign of alarm.

But Patrick saunters out of the store, no problem. He's wearing a smile as wide as the Saint Lawrence River. He unzips his jacket to show us...

"A video game! Wow! POP!"

"Shhh!" said Clementine. "Not so loud!"

She's trembling in fear. She didn't approve of this plan. But all the others are impressed with Patrick's feat.

"Your turn now, CHIEF!" says Patrick snidely.

The others look at me in silence. I can't back down now.

So I turn into a Patrick clone again. Just do it, don't think about it. Act tough.

"Not a very good choice!" I sneer. "Everyone already has that video game."

I turn my back and march resolutely into the store. If Patrick can do it, it can't be too hard. I just have to do the same thing he did.

I stop at a counter here and there, pretending to browse. I pick up an object and examine it as if it really interests me. But I don't see a thing. My mouth is dry, my hands are clammy.

I am sure that everyone knows what I'm up to. I quickly put the object back in place. I mustn't stay in one spot too long. That looks suspicious.

I go over to another counter. It's not any better. I'm so nervous that every move I make must look suspicious.

I'll never do it. I wish I could just leave. But then I think of the others and how they'll make fun of me. "Maddie's chicken!"

Piles of tee-shirts spill over the counter in front of me. I have only to reach out my hand. I'll take the red one...no, the yellow one. It's pretty!

I want the tee-shirt, and that makes me less afraid. I glance quickly around me. A few people are walking by quickly. Over there, an old lady is trying on gloves. She's not looking my way. Now!

But once I make my mind up, I'm scared again. My hand is shaking and I just grab any old tee-shirt. I slip it into my jacket. Then I turn tail.

Inside me a voice is yelling, "Don't rush! You're attracting attention. Slow down!"

The exit seems to be kilometres away. I can feel the tee-shirt slipping under my jacket. My heart is beating so fast it will probably push the tee-shirt out.

Now the door is near. My friends are waiting. I can see them staring at me, wide-eyed. Through my fear I feel a stab of satisfaction. They're really impressed! But now — what's the matter?

They take a step back...another...now they're running away. At that very instant, a hand comes down on my shoulder.

5
Little orphan Maddie

Someone is unzipping my jacket and pulling out the tee-shirt. I hear voices. In my head. Outside me. I can't tell anymore. "Caught you. Caught you. Thief!"

My whole body turns numb. It's as if it's trying to escape reality.

"...have to follow me..."

I feel myself lifted up and dragged along. I can't escape. Reality is HUGE. All the customers in the store are staring at me. I know it.

Other voices echo in my ears. "Disgraceful! Put her in jail... only what she deserves."

Then, the silence of a small dark room. My captor releases me. He leaves the room before I even see him.

I keep my eyes lowered. A stern male voice orders me to sit down.

I collapse onto a chair. My bones have turned to water. The only thing keeping me up is the electric shocks going through my body.

"What you did is a very serious matter. Very serious."

The police will be sent for. They'll handcuff me and take me to jail. My picture will be in the paper and everyone in the

whole world will know that I am a criminal.

No, no, I'm not! It's not true. I'm a good little girl.

"I'm not really a criminal," I sob. "It was a contest for a democratic election. And...I'm against violence, I'm against war. I'm too young to go to — boohoohoo — sniff —"

"You should have thought about that beforehand! But... I'm willing to give you a chance. Perhaps you have already been punished enough."

I feel like a drowning person who has come up into the air. I begin to breathe a bit more easily.

"We'll have to phone your parents."

GULP! I'm going back under.

My parents will never trust me again. They'll watch every little thing I do. It will be impossible.

They're still mad at me for stealing Julian's french fries, and that was months ago. If they find out that I shoplifted, I'll never hear the end of it!

"I — I don't have any parents! I'm an orphan."

"I see. And who looks after you?"

"Uh...my grandmother."

Gran will understand. I know she will. The democratic election was her idea anyway.

I give the man her phone number. He calls her and explains the situation to her coldly. He's so mean! This must be a terrible shock for Gran.

The man seems concerned. "Hello? Are you still there?"

A few minutes go by. I am seized with a new terror. I can see Gran lying on the ground — dead. And all because of me. Now I really am a criminal.

"She's on her way," the man tells me as he hangs up the phone.

He seems as relieved as I am. I have never lived through so many horrors in a single hour. And all because of a tee-shirt I didn't even want.

The tee-shirt is lying on the table in front of me. It's brown, and the ugliest thing you ever saw. I wouldn't be caught dead in it.

There's a knock on the door. Can it be Gran already?

No, it's another old lady. But...I recognize her! She's the one who was trying on gloves when I grabbed the tee-shirt. What's she doing here?

Another shock for me! She takes off her grey wig and her old coat. Before my eyes, she is transformed.

"My shift's over, sir," she says. "Nothing else to report."

She's the one who got me arrested! The store detective was disguised as a little old lady. Can you believe it?

Sometimes people really aren't very...honest.

6
Back from Hell

Gran wrote a note for my teacher and took me back to school.

"I'll see you this afternoon, for our bicycle training," she said.

I wasn't looking forward to it. Gran would be angry with me for sure. But I'd rather have Gran mad at me than go to jail. What a close call! I just barely escaped that nightmare.

At recess the gang surrounded me and bombarded me with whispered questions.

They seemed impressed. I started to feel better. After a

dramatic pause, to let the sus-
pense build, I declared, "I have
just returned from Hell. This is
an experience I would not wish
for any of you. It demands
nerves of steel."

"Weren't you scared?"

"Uh...the important thing is
to master your fear. I was in-
terrogated, grilled. But I was
able to convince them of my
innocence."

"How did you do that?
They're the innocent ones!'

"I told them the truth!"

Before my eyes, Patrick
turned into a boiled potato, all
pale and mushy. If I peeled him,
he'd fall into pieces. I could
mash him. But I wouldn't do
that.

"Don't worry. I didn't tell on you. I didn't mention any of you. You would have been considered accomplices."

Their eyes widened in terror. None of them would ever bring up this incident again.

"A chief has to protect the members of her gang," I added.

Then the bell rang. Recess was over. The elections would have to be held tomorrow. I figured I had a better chance of winning than I did this morning.

So, really, every cloud has a silver lining, even when you go through Hell.

* * *

When I got home, the silver lining started to tarnish. Do you know what my mother said?

"I want to take you to All for You. You need some new clothes."

"Noooo! I don't need anything!"

I'm never again setting foot in that store, and especially not with my parents along! I would be terrified of being recognized.

My mother was puzzled. She couldn't understand why I didn't want to go shopping. I acted indignant.

"It's more important to train with Gran than to go shopping. Here's Gran now!"

Out of the frying pan, into the fire. What if Gran told my mom?

But no, she kept the secret. Still, my troubles weren't over.

Gran didn't say a word as we left the house. I felt very uncomfortable as we rode along. I was suffocating. A voice inside me was begging her, "Talk to me!"

She stopped pedalling abruptly, just as if she had heard me.

"I know you don't feel good about yourself," she said.

But she didn't try to comfort me. Instead she scolded me.

"You were a coward. If the gang had asked you to steal something from ME, would you have done it? How far would

you go to impress your friends? It would have shown true courage if you had said no."

I started to cry. Gran softened a little, but continued her lecture.

"Maddie, I don't think you deserve to be chief. It's because of leaders like you that wars break out. Leaders who will do anything for power, even crush democracy and fight with their brothers if they vote against them"

I thought of Alexander. I was ashamed, just like yesterday.

"What should I do, Gran?" I stammered.

"You'll have to decide that yourself," she answered. "If you really understand, you'll make the right decision."

All I understood right then was that Gran still trusted me. It was a tiny ray of light in the blackness surrounding me. I didn't want it to go out.

* * *

First I made up with Alexander.

"I'll vote for you," he promised.

"So will I," said Julian, squeezing my hand.

Even a little genius can be scared to go into the schoolyard for the first time. I told both of them that they wouldn't need to vote for me.

As soon as everyone in the gang was together, I announced the news.

"I'm resigning as chief. Instead I nominate...Clementine. She has everything we need in a chief. She's the best one in the class, she's the smartest, AND she's the strongest."

After a moment of astonished silence, the gang broke into applause and unanimously elected Clementine by acclamation.

She'll be a good chief, to judge from her first decision.

"You're taking the video game back to the store," she told

Patrick. "We're not going to have any thieves in our gang."

Finally, I feel happy with myself again. I'll never try to be like anyone else again. I don't want to go back to that nightmare. No way! I couldn't wait to tell Gran.

"I don't agree," Julian protested suddenly. "Maddie should be the chief. Billions of blistering blue barnacles!"

Julian really is a little genius....You know why? Because Clementine always does what I want.

Meet six other great kids in the New First Novels Series!

• Meet Duff the Daring
in *Duff the Giant Killer*
by Budge Wilson/Illustrated by Kim LaFave
Getting over the chicken pox can be boring, but Duff and Simon find a great way to enjoy themselves — acting out one of their favourite stories, *Jack the Giant Killer*, in the park. In fact, they do it so well the police get into the act.

• Meet Jan the Curious
in *Jan's Big Bang*
by Monica Hughes/Illustrated by Carlos Freire
Taking part in the Science Fair is a big deal for Grade Three kids, but Jan and her best friend Sarah are ready for the challenge. Still, finding a safe project isn't easy, and the girls discover that getting ready for the fair can cause a whole lot of trouble.

• Meet Carrie the Courageous
in *Go For It, Carrie*
by Lesley Choyce/ Illustrated by Mark Thurman
More than anything else, Carrie wants to roller-blade. Her big brother and his friend just laugh at her. But Carrie knows she can do it if she just keeps trying. As her friend Gregory tells her, "You can do it, Carrie. Go for it!"

• Meet Lilly the Bossy
in *Lilly to the Rescue*
by Brenda Bellingham/ Illustrated by Kathy Kaulbach

Bossy-boots! That's what kids at school start calling Lilly when she gives a lot of advice that's not wanted. Lilly can't help telling people what to do — but how can she keep any of her friends if she always knows better?

• Meet Morgan the Magician
in *Morgan Makes Magic*
by Ted Staunton/Illustrated by Bill Slavin

When he's in a tight spot, Morgan tells stories — and most of them stretch the truth, to say the least. But when he tells kids at his new school he can do magic tricks, he really gets in trouble — most of all with the dreaded Aldeen Hummel!

• Meet Robyn the Dreamer
in *Shoot for the Moon, Robyn*
by Hazel Hutchins/Illustrated by Yvonne Cathcart

When the teacher asks her to sing for the class, Robyn knows it's her chance to be the world's best singer. Should she perform like Celine Dion, or do *My Bonnie Lies Over the Ocean*, or the matchmaker song? It's hard to decide, even for the world's best singer — and the three boys who throw spitballs don't make it any easier.

Look for these First Novels!

Formac Publishing Company Limited
5502 Atlantic Street, Halifax, Nova Scotia B3H 1G4
Orders: 1-800-565-1975 Fax: (902) 425-0166

—